# SUPER®

## takes on
## One-Sided Sid,
## Un-Wonderer®
### and the
### Team of Unthinkables©

WRITTEN BY:

**MICHELLE GARCIA WINNER**

**STEPHANIE MADRIGAL**

ILLUSTRATED BY:

**KYLE RICHARDSON**

Social Thinking jr

©2013 Social Thinking Publishing
San Jose, CA

MW01056676

**Superflex® Takes on One-Sided Sid©, Un-Wonderer© and the Team of Unthinkables©**

Stephanie Madrigal, Speech Language Pathologist, MA, CCC-SLP, and
Michelle Garcia Winner, Speech Language Pathologist, MA, CCC-SLP

Edited by Sandy Horwich, sandra@shorwich.com

Illustrations and Graphic Design by Kyle Richardson, info@bornonthefrontier.com

Copyright© 2013, Social Thinking Publishing.
All rights reserved. This book may not be copied in its entirety for any reason.
The following terms are trademarked and/or copyrighted by Social Thinking Publishing:
    Social Thinking®
    Superflex®
    Team of Unthinkables©
    Each of the Unthinkables' names are also copyrighted

Library of Congress Control Number: 2013949106

ISBN: 978-0-9701320-5-5

Social Thinking Publishing
3031 Tisch Way, Suite 800
San Jose, CA 95128
Phone: (877) 464-9278
Fax: (408) 557-8594

This book is printed and bound in Tennessee by Mighty Color.

**Books can be ordered online at www.socialthinking.com.**

## Advance Praise for
## Superflex Takes on One-Sided Sid, Un-Wonderer
## and the Team of Unthinkables

"A 'smorgasbord' of material for teaching some of the most challenging aspects of social learning: showing interest in others and flexible thinking. It will keep you coming back for more!"

-Beckham L., SLP

"Thanks Superflex Academy once again! This book is packed with loads of strategies to tackle key Social Thinking concepts in FUN, easy to read and practical ways. I love teaching my students to use the Interest-O-Meter to support their thinking to defeat One-Sided Sid and Un-Wonderer."

-DM, Special Educator

"This book creatively embeds many Social Thinking concepts throughout, using both text and illustrations. I'm eager to join my students as we enjoy and absorb the rich content hidden inside."

-Linda M., CCC-SLP

This comic book is dedicated to all the citizens who keep working every day to improve their superflexible thinking powers and defeat those sneaky Unthinkables!

# TABLE OF CONTENTS

**1**

**2**

**3**

# One Step at a Time!

## Cautions and Information About the Use of This Material

*Superflex Takes on One-Sided Sid, Un-Wonderer and the Team of Unthinkables* is book four of our Superflex comic book series. This series is designed to help children learn more about their own social behavior and strategies to regulate it. As charming and captivating as Superflex and the Team of Unthinkables are to students, this is *not* a starting place for teaching them about Social Thinking and social behavior change. Social Thinking Vocabulary and related concepts need to be first introduced to help children explore what it means to think social, to give them a common vocabulary to discuss these sometimes complex concepts and understand the relationship between social thinking and social behavioral expectations.

To be used effectively, parents and educators need to start at the beginning, introduce core concepts, and work through the Superflex curriculum *before* sharing this comic book (or others to follow) with children. Books should be introduced in this order:

1. *You Are a Social Detective!*
2. *Superflex... A Superhero Social Thinking Curriculum*
3. *Superflex Takes on Rock Brain and the Team of Unthinkables* (packaged with the Superflex Curriculum book)
4. *Social Town Citizens Discover 82 New Unthinkables for Superflex to Outsmart! (Introducing Superflex's Very Cool Five-Step Power Plan and the Thinkables©)*

Once these four books have been used with a child or class, adults are free to move on to any of the individual Unthinkables books we have produced to date, in any order that meets the child's social thinking challenges or interests:

- *Superflex Takes on Glassman and the Team of Unthinkables*
- *Superflex Takes on Brain Eater and the Team of Unthinkables*
- *Superflex Takes on One-Sided Sid, Un-Wonderer and the Team of Unthinkables*

In *You Are a Social Detective*, children are introduced – through child-friendly illustrations and language – to core concepts that make up the Social Thinking curriculum, such as "expected" and "unexpected" behavior, "school smarts" versus "social smarts" and other relevant concepts. Engaging lessons make social thinking come alive for children.

*Superflex...A Superhero Social Thinking Curriculum* introduces Superflex, a social thinking superhero who helps the citizens of Social Town outsmart the Team of Unthinkables and diminish their powers to distract, disengage, and otherwise detour children in their efforts to think about others and use their social thinking abilities. Fun worksheets motivate students to learn more about how their brain works; concrete strategies give them tools to become better social thinkers.

In *Superflex Takes on Rock Brain and the Team of Unthinkables*, children are exposed to their first Unthinkable character as they work through the Superflex Curriculum. This foundation of learning sets the stage for them to then move onto other books in the series, such as Glassman or Brain Eater. Each comic book highlights a particular Unthinkable and its powers while teaching readers about strategies they can use to defeat their own Unthinkables. The book, *Social Town Citizens Discover 82 New Unthinkables for Superflex to Outsmart!*, introduces more characters and a new Five-Step Power Plan for students to add to their Superflexible thinking tool box.

The ultimate goal of all Social Thinking teachings is to help children become better observers of social information and improve their ability to self-regulate their social behavioral responses within the natural settings where they share space and possibly interact with others.

Adults can learn more about the Social Thinking model, along with additional teaching strategies, in the book, *Think Social* (Winner, 2005). Many free articles, blogs and information about additional resources can be found at www.socialthinking.com.

## About This Book

In *Superflex Takes on One-Sided Sid, Un-Wonderer and the Team of Unthinkables*, children become familiar with several ways to get the better of One-Sided Sid and his sidekick sister Un-Wonderer when they try to get students to do or say things that show they're only thinking about themselves and not others. Although the story introduces specific strategies, such as using people files to keep track of what others like to talk about, it's recommended that adults also explore the references at the back of the book. These provide additional resources for expanded discussions with children and students.

Not all strategies presented in the book will apply to every child. Caregivers and educators should closely evaluate what strategies work best for each child and encourage children to identify what strategies they do and don't like.

The authors recognize that other strategies exist that can be used to help students learn to show interest in others. Social Thinking is not a stand-alone teaching curriculum and integrates well with other methods. The authors encourage adults to brainstorm ideas with team members as well as explore other resources and the Internet for additional tools and ideas that may help their students.

## Using the Series: Things to Keep in Mind

- Children who will benefit from the Superflex curriculum are those who can differentiate well between fantasy and reality. They are encouraged to think about and understand that Superflex is a pretend character. The students must also be able to imagine they have a Superflexible superhero within them that can help them identify and use strategies to change their behavior. This is a very different concept than pretending to be a superhero in a play situation. Children who struggle with these ideas may not be good candidates for the Superflex curriculum.

- The concepts in this book are best suited for all third to fifth graders and are particularly helpful for students with social learning challenges. Many classroom teachers and elementary school principals have adopted Superflex into their curriculum for typically developing children in Kindergarten to second grade. However, the more advanced concepts in Superflex, such as using strategies to change their own "unthinkable behavior" may be too complex a learning process for our younger students (four to eight years old) with social learning challenges.

- Not all students will benefit from this curriculum. Discontinue its use if students get stuck solely focusing on the Team of Unthinkables or argue that they don't want to develop a Superflexible part of their brain.

- We often find that students who struggle to learn specific Social Thinking concepts may benefit from these same lessons one or two years later as they acquire more self-reflective maturity.

## Learning is Fun!

The purpose of the Superflex products is to provide educators, teachers or parents with a fun, motivating and nonthreatening way to help students explore social thinking while increasing their knowledge of social expectations, their own social behavior and learning ways to modify their behaviors using Superflexible strategies.

Experiential learning activities, via handouts and lessons, are an important part of the social learning curriculum. Included with this book is a CD that contains lessons to further teach these concepts to children. Many lessons address people files. These files are a way to help students think about taking what they learn about others and storing it in their brain. Students learn how to gather information by asking questions and by observation. The students have a chance to create various people files about some of the Superflex students and people in their own Social Town.

Some lessons include extra credit and extra extra credit tasks. These questions require students to put the concepts discussed in the lesson into action at school, in the community or at home. This helps generalize social thinking and social learning into all areas of a student's life.

**Welcome!** If you're reading this story, you've probably been chosen to be a student at the National Superflex Academy. Superflex will be your teacher and Bark, his dog, is his assistant. Superflex teaches us that we all have the power of Superflex inside our own brains.

By going to the Academy with us, you'll have special lessons to help defeat the powers of two very special Unthinkables, One-Sided Sid and Un-Wonderer! When these two pranksters take over your brain, they make you do and say things that show you aren't thinking about others or how they feel.

But before we go any further with stripping these guys of their powers, we need to make sure we know the basics!

1

To make your own Superflex's power stronger, it's important for you to learn as much as you can about each of the Unthinkables. This will help you know which Unthinkables might be trying to take over your own Superflex power.

Bark wants you to make sure you know that at the Academy you have to learn *strategies*. Strategies are special thinking tools you can use when any Unthinkable is trying to take charge of your brain power.

During this story, quizzes will test how you're doing in developing your Superflex smarts. (Hint: You can look on the last pages of the book to see possible answers. But try your best first before peeking!)

The Team of Unthinkables has been around a long time, invading and controlling the brains of the citizens in Social Town! In Social Town, people just like you live together and think about each other every day.

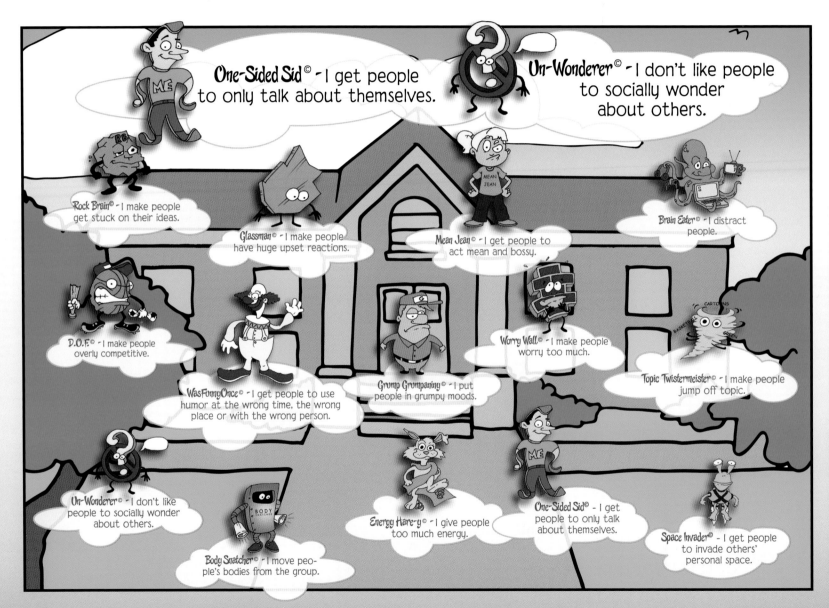

We've just heard that One-Sided Sid and his sister Un-Wonderer are on the loose and invading the brains of Social Town citizens.

You see, One-Sided Sid changes our citizens' thinking when they're in a conversation so they only think and talk about themselves.

Un-Wonderer will do her best to stop people from having Social Wonders about others.

5

## One-Sided Sid
I like to make people talk only about their own interests or themselves!

It's okay to tell people bits of information about yourself — we all like to tell people about ourselves! But when One-Sided Sid and his sister take over, look out! The sharing gets all out of balance! When that happens, people around you may think you aren't interested in thinking about them. That makes them feel bad.

**Un-Wonderer**
I like to keep people from thinking about others!

They may also think you don't want to let them talk about what they like to talk about! In this adventure, you'll learn ways to keep thinking about other people when you hang out, talk or play with them. Then you'll have more strategies to help defeat the amazingly strong powers of One-Sided Sid, Un-Wonderer and some of their Unthinkable friends.

CITIZENS ARE REPORTING THEY FEEL LONELIER LATELY. AT FIRST, VERY FEW CITIZENS NOTICED THEY WEREN'T INTERESTED IN WHAT OTHER CITIZENS HAD TO SAY.

BUT WHEN THE FAMOUS MOVIE STAR, EMMIE WINNER, CAME TO VISIT SOCIAL TOWN, SHE NOTICED RIGHT AWAY THAT NO ONE SEEMED TO SHOW ANY INTEREST IN OTHERS... OR EVEN IN HER! THAT MADE HER WANT TO LEAVE RIGHT AWAY!

Famous actress wants to leave Social Town!

SOCIAL TOWN CHANNEL 4 NEWS

When people think only about themselves, they talk only about themselves and their own interests. They don't even notice when other people aren't listening to them anymore! That's no fun for anyone. When you see that happening, it's probably One-Sided Sid and Un-Wonderer taking over their brains. It can happen to everyone – even you!

The Social Town News camera crews captured this scene when Emmie Winner visited Social Town.

## Quiz #1:

What do the Unthinkables One-Sided Sid and Un-Wonderer do to take over a citizen's thinking?

# Chapter 3:
# THE UNTHINKABLES TAKE OVER SOCIAL TOWN ELEMENTARY!

**Welcome to the Social Town Elementary Spelling Bee!**
Today's winner will represent Social Town at the National Spelling Bee Championship.

When Katie wins the Spelling Bee at school, many of her classmates congratulate her and ask her questions about the championship. But Thomas doesn't congratulate Katie or talk to her when the Spelling Bee is over.

Aiden hopes Thomas can remember his strategies to defeat his Unthinkables.

13

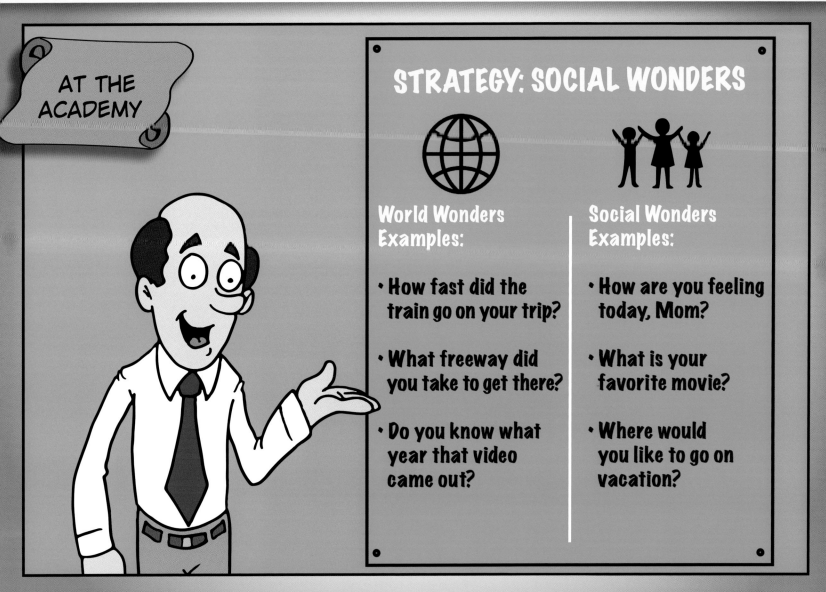

AT THE ACADEMY

## STRATEGY: SOCIAL WONDERS

**World Wonders Examples:**

- How fast did the train go on your trip?

- What freeway did you take to get there?

- Do you know what year that video came out?

**Social Wonders Examples:**

- How are you feeling today, Mom?

- What is your favorite movie?

- Where would you like to go on vacation?

The Superflex Academy teacher begins his lesson on the Social Wonder strategy. The kids will learn the difference between Social Wonders and World Wonders.

The teacher plays a video of kids using their Social Wonder strategy. "Wondering and being curious about what people tell you and figuring out what you don't know about what they did is a great start to thinking about them," the teacher says. "It also keeps One-Sided Sid and Un-Wonderer from taking over."

"You can practice wondering about what others are telling you and what you don't know. Then you can turn some of the wonders into social wonder questions. This might take some practice, but you can do it." Superflex and Bark are happy teachers! This lesson on Social Wonders is important!

The Academy students took a minute to practice thinking up Social Wonders about people in their lives. Then they wrote Social Wonder questions they could ask those people. The teacher proudly looks at all their great questions and sends them on their way to their next class.

## Quiz #2:

What kinds of Wonders are the following examples – World Wonder or Social Wonder?

a) Why is taffy sticky?

b) Which country has the most islands?

c) What's Grandma's favorite book?

d) What does your teacher like to do in her spare time for fun?

e) Where was racquetball invented?

f) How are things going with your friend and his new puppy?

Superflex and Bark know there are some more strategies to defeat the sneaky powers of One-Sided Sid and Un-Wonderer. Here they check in and listen about another strategy students can use.

**WAYS TO HELP OTHERS FEEL GOOD**

1. We show we're interested in others by connecting to what they're talking about.

2. We remember things about other people's lives, such as their favorite sports team or singer, or the name of their pet.

3. We ask people questions about things we remember they like. For example, if you remember someone's sports team, you might ask her: "Have you been watching their games on TV?"

WE'VE LEARNED IN ALL OF OUR YEARS OF STUDYING SOCIAL THINKING THAT PEOPLE ARE MORE LIKELY TO WANT TO BE WITH US IF WE HELP THEM TO FEEL GOOD. LET'S LOOK AT WAYS WE CAN DO THIS.

Sometimes the tricky part is knowing what to talk about or to ask. Your memory can help a lot in this situation. We've created some strategies to help us use our social memory. One strategy is called a people file.

When we see someone who we've met before, our brain tries to locate the people file on that person and open it. Once inside the people file, we can start to remember what we thought that person liked to talk about. This helps us remember what topics that person likes to talk about and what questions we can ask to show we remember information about the person.

Let's watch some videos of these strategies in action. Frank is using his people file to remember what he knows about Juan. This will help him think of something to talk about.

*Quiz #3:*

What information do you have in your people file for your mom? Your dad? Your teacher? A classmate? A friend?

Jillian does a nice job of remembering something about her friend and asking her a question about it. This makes Frances feel great.

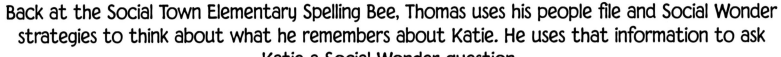

Back at the Social Town Elementary Spelling Bee, Thomas uses his people file and Social Wonder strategies to think about what he remembers about Katie. He uses that information to ask Katie a Social Wonder question.

28

One-Sided Sid and Un-Wonderer are getting worried they are not strong enough to control Social Town citizens! Time to work even harder at the gym!

29

Luckily, Aiden's mom, Mrs. Cruz and the school principal know about Aiden's Superflexible training powers. If the Superflex Brain Sensor goes off and Aiden needs to leave class to help a citizen, he just needs to tell Mrs. Cruz.

ATTENTION SUPERFLEX: MARY, A STUDENT AT SCHOOL, IS HAVING AN UNTHINKABLE MOMENT IN THE CAFETERIA. ONE-SIDED SID AND UN-WONDERER ARE TEAMING UP TO CHANGE HER THINKING. SHE'S WITH KIDS FROM CLASS BUT SHE'S ONLY THINKING ABOUT HERSELF AND ONLY TALKING ABOUT WHAT SHE WANTS TO TALK ABOUT.

Mary is only talking about what SHE is interested in! She isn't thinking or wondering about anyone else — what they think, what they might want to talk about or how they feel. She's showing NO interest in them at all!

35

Keeping people interested in us is tricky! There are times each of us bores other people, at least a little. This is expected.

When we don't think about others and just talk about ourselves, One-Sided Sid and Un-Wonderer can sneak into our brains and gain power!

**Quiz #4:**

What are some clues that we might see if people probably
are NOT INTERESTED in what we're saying?

We can look for signs or clues in people to decide if they're bored with what we're saying, or interested in what we're talking about. We listen to what they say, and we can also look at their body language.

### *Quiz #5:*

Think about yourself when One-Sided Sid and Un-Wonderer have power in your brain. What are two strategies you can try to use to take their powers away?

The students write down their homework assignment and pack up for their next class. In this class, they'll learn about two more strategies that are sure to help when One-Sided Sid and Un-Wonderer show up. The two strategies are Add-a-Thought and Ask-a-Question.

The students now work with Mrs. Wagner. She's been at the school for 15 years and knows all there is to know about how to defeat One-Sided Sid and Un-Wonderer.

44

45

NOW LET'S LEARN ABOUT OUR ASK-A-QUESTION STRATEGY. IT TAKES SOME PRACTICE BUT IS WELL WORTH IT.

FIRST, LET'S GO OVER THE QUESTION WORDS THAT HELP US THINK ABOUT THE QUESTIONS WE CAN ASK.

# Who, What, Where, When, Why, and How

**Example:**

**Dan:** "I am going to New York city with my mom this weekend."

**Jeff:** "Cool. WHAT fun things are you gonna do there?"

or

**Jeff:** "WHERE will you be staying?"

or

**Jeff:** "WHY are you going to New York?"

"HOW are you getting there?"

"WHEN are you getting back?"

47

The teacher has the students practice their Add-a-Thought strategy and Ask-a-Question strategy with Ricky the Robo-Citizen.

Ricky is talking about the trip he just took to the Grand Canyon.

The teacher now leads them into the Interest-O-Meter Center where they'll learn about a new strategy to help them detect how interested people are during a conversation.

**Quiz #6:**

True or False: Our Interest-O-Meter should stay turned off in the classroom because we're expected to pay attention and learn even if it gets boring once in a while.

The teacher explains that if the Interest-O-Meter stays too long on the orange or red level, it's in the social danger zone. When that happens, it's possible that One-Sided Sid and Un-Wonderer are gaining power!

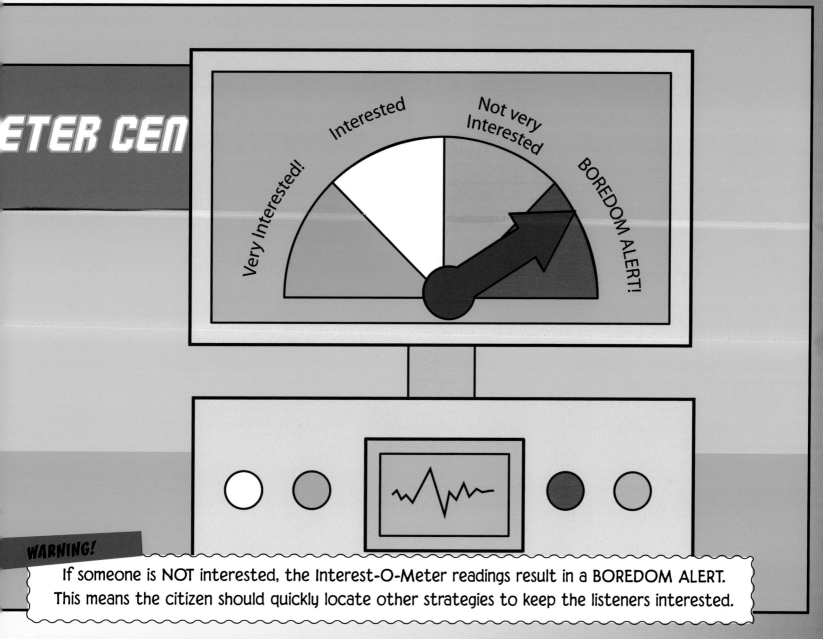

**WARNING!**

If someone is NOT interested, the Interest-O-Meter readings result in a BOREDOM ALERT. This means the citizen should quickly locate other strategies to keep the listeners interested.

The teacher asks the students to get into groups so they can practice turning on and using the Interest-O-Meters. By training their brain with this tool and practicing, they hope to notice these clues when talking to others around Social Town.

Chapter 10:
BEING FLEXIBLE: CAN SHE DO IT?

60

61

When Mary showed she was thinking about her friends and that she was interested in them, they all had good feelings about her. That made them want to be around her.

63

64

The SF Academy teachers have put together some fun materials for you to learn more about how to create people files and how to ask a question based on the information in your people file. Remember to practice your strategies and help defeat the powers of One-Sided Sid and his sidekick sister, Un-Wonderer!

BRAIN EATER

# Superflex's Top-Secret Tip Sheet to Defeat the Team of Unthinkables!

GLASSMAN

**Glassman:** Turn your body and eyes away from the item that is distracting, and focus on what someone is telling you.

ROCK BRAIN

**Rock Brain:** Take a deep breath and remember that you always have a different choice. Think about your choices, and choose one that helps others to feel good.

BODY SNATCHER

**Body Snatcher:** Remember to point your shoulders toward the group and keep your body about one arm's length away from other people if you are standing near them.

DOF

**DOF, the Destroyer of Fun:** Self-talk: "If I stay calm and remind myself that everyone has to take turns getting their way, then people call me a "good sport." Then others will want to play with me."

UN-WONDERER

**Un-Wonderer:** Create a "people file" in my brain about people I know. When I see them later, remember what I know about them and ask questions about what they like to do.

SPACE INVADER

**Space Invader:** Use the one-arm rule to see if you are standing too close – which means you are supposed to stand about one arm's length from people. If you stand closer, they start to feel really uncomfortable!

ENERGY HARE-Y

**Energy Hare-y:** Look around with your eyes and see if your energy level matches those around you. In class, everyone's bodies are calm, so if your body is busier, take a couple of deep breaths to calm it down.

GRUMP GRUMPANINY

**Grump-Grumpaniny:** Use your Inner Coach: "If I stay positive with my words, my friends around me will want to keep talking to me and will have good thoughts about me."

ONE SIDED SID

**One-Sided Sid:** When you are with your friends, try to ask them questions about topics they like to talk about. You can try to remember something they told you the last time you were with them and ask them about it. This will make them feel good and think that you are interested in them.

CARS

DOG

YELLOW

TOPIC TWISTERMEISTER

**Topic Twistermeister:** Listen to what people are talking about, and ask questions about what they are saying even if you really want to talk about your own interests.

WORRY WALL

**Worry Wall:** Find a thought that can change your worried thought to a calm thought: "Oh, this math problem looks too hard. But I can always ask for help from my teacher."

WAS FUNNY ONCE

**WasFunnyOnce:** Self-talk: "Is now a silly moment, or a learning moment? If it is a learning moment (most of the time in class), then I can keep my silly thought in my head so my teacher can keep teaching."

MEAN JEAN

**Mean Jean:** Self-talk: "These bossy words might hurt my friend's feelings, so I can keep those thoughts in my head. She does not need me to tell her what to do."

# Superflex Quiz Answers

There are many correct responses and possible answers to the quizzes you've taken throughout the book. So don't worry if your answers don't match the ones below. Superflex just wants to give you some ideas and choices to think about.

## Superflex Quiz #1:

What do the Unthinkables One-Sided Sid and Un-Wonderer do to take over a citizen's thinking?

Possible answers: One-Sided Sid gets people to only think and talk about themselves and what they want to talk and think about. Un-Wonderer keeps people from having Social Wonders about others.

## Superflex Quiz #2:

What kinds of Wonders are the following examples - World Wonders or Social Wonders?
a) Why is taffy sticky? **World Wonder**
b) Which country has the most islands? **World Wonder**
c) What's Grandma's favorite book? **Social Wonder**
d) What does your teacher like to do in her spare time for fun? **Social Wonder**
e) Where was racquetball invented? **World Wonder**
f) How are things going with your friend and his new puppy? **Social Wonder**

## Superflex Quiz #3:

What information do you have in your people file for your mom? Your dad? Your teacher? A classmate? A friend?
Possible answers: Answers will vary but they all should be about the person you've chosen.

## Superflex Quiz #4:

What are some clues that we might see if people probably are NOT INTERESTED in what we're saying?
Possible answers: Not adding thoughts, not asking questions, trying to change the topic, looking away, body facing away from us, not talking at all.

## Superflex Quiz #5:

Think about yourself when One-Sided Sid and Un-Wonderer have power in your brain. What are two strategies you can try to use to take their powers away?

Possible answers: Adding a thought, adding a comment, asking a Social Wonder question, opening up a people file on the person we're talking to.

## Superflex Quiz #6:

True or False? Our Interest-O-Meter should stay turned off in the classroom because we're expected to pay attention and learn even if it gets boring once in a while.

Possible answers: True (most of the time). Our Interest-O-Meter switch should be turned off in the classroom while the teacher is teaching. We can turn it on and use it carefully when we're doing group work with others. It can be turned on mainly when we're around our classmates and friends talking.

## Additional Resources

Find more lessons developed by Social Thinking related to the following topics introduced in this comic book:

## People Files and Social Memory

Winner, M. (2007). *Thinking About YOU, Thinking About ME*. San Jose, CA: Think Social Publishing, Inc., page 58.

Winner, M. (2005). *Think Social*. San Jose, CA: Think Social Publishing, Inc., page 239.

## Social Wonders vs World Wonders

Winner, M. (2005). *Think Social*. San Jose, CA: Think Social Publishing, Inc. In Section 6: Adjusting our Participation and Language Based on What Other People are Thinking, Imagining and Wondering, pages 181-238.

## Observing Others for Clues and Becoming A Social Detective

Winner, M. & Crooke, P. (2010). *You Are A Social Detective: Explaining Social Thinking To Kids*. San Jose, CA: Think Social Publishing, Inc.

## Using Language to Show Interest in Others

Winner, M. (2007). *Thinking About YOU, Thinking About ME*. San Jose, CA: Think Social Publishing, Inc. In Chapter 7: Using Language to Develop and Sustain Relationships, pages 115-150.

Winner, M. (2005). *Think Social*. San Jose, CA: Think Social Publishing, Inc. In Section 7: Our Language Makes Others Have Different Thoughts and Feelings, pages 243-311.

# The Superflex Series!

### You Are a Social Detective!
Michelle Garcia Winner and Pamela Crooke

For parents and professionals to use with students 4 years - 5th grade

Every one of us is a Social Detective. We are good Social Detectives when we use our eyes, ears, and brains to figure out what others mean by their words and deeds and are planning to do next. This entertaining comic book teaches children how to develop their own skills and become successful Social Detectives!

### Superflex... A Superhero Social Thinking Curriculum*
Stephanie Madrigal and Michelle Garcia Winner

### Superflex Takes on Rock Brain and the Team of Unthinkables*
Stephanie Madrigal

For professionals and parents to use with students in 2nd - 5th grade

The Superflex Curriculum offers educators, parents, and therapists fun and motivating ways to help students with social and communication difficulties develop an awareness of their own social thinking and behaviors, then learn self-regulation strategies across a range of these behaviors.

Through a comic book format, students are introduced to Superflex, a superhero who lives inside each child, and Rock Brain, one of the Team of Unthinkables, characters that try to detour students from using their social thinking skills. Rock Brain makes kids get stuck on their ideas. Creative strategies to defeat Rock Brain are included.

*Packaged and sold as a set; Curriculum includes CD with lessons and funwork.

### Superflex Takes on Glassman and the Team of Unthinkables
Stephanie Madrigal and Michelle Garcia Winner

For professionals and parents to use with students in K - 5th grade

In this teaching comic book, Superflex swoops down to help Aiden overcome the Unthinkable, Glassman, who causes children to have over-sized reactions to small things. The setting: the first day of school!

# Of Related Interest

### Whole Body Listening Larry at Home
### Whole Body Listening Larry at School
Both books by Kristen Wilson and Elizabeth Sautter

For parents and professionals to use with students 4-9 years old

These colorfully illustrated storybooks provide fun ways to teach younger children an abstract but essential idea - that their eyes, hands, brains — their whole bodies! — communicate, engage with and affect the people around them. Scenarios range from at home and at school to in the car, with friends or grandparents.

**All titles available at the Social Thinking website: www.socialthinking.com**

## Core Books About the Social Thinking Model & Related Teaching Strategies

### Inside Out: What Makes a Person with Social Cognitive Deficits Tick?
By Michelle Garcia Winner

For professionals and parents to use with all ages!

The starting place to learn about the ILAUGH Model upon which Social Thinking is based. Discusses the direct connection between social thinking and academic problems such as reading comprehension and written expression, and helps readers pinpoint specific challenges in a child or student. Valuable insight on information we expect students to know to become strong learners but that doesn't develop "naturally" in everyone.

### Thinking About YOU Thinking About ME, 2nd Edition
By Michelle Garcia Winner

For professionals and parents to use with all ages!

Learn more about social interaction and social awareness! Explains Michelle Garcia Winner's core Social Thinking concepts and treatment methods, with extensive curriculum content on perspective taking as well as assessment using the Social Thinking Dynamic Assessment Protocol®. Age-targeted lesson and activity ideas, templates and handouts included. A precursor to using books like **Superflex, You Are A Social Detective,** and more!

### Think Social!
### A Social Thinking Curriculum for School-Aged Students, 2nd Edition
By Michelle Garcia Winner

For parents and professionals to use with all ages!

A complement to **Thinking About YOU Thinking About ME,** this is the fundamental Social Thinking curriculum book to help individuals K-12 and into adulthood. The book sequences through eight chapters and 69 lessons that help students explore the basics of working and thinking in a group. Each chapter addresses how to use and interpret language (verbal and nonverbal) to further understand the context of communications.

**Social Thinking books, curriculum, worksheets, and related products developed by Michelle Garcia Winner and Social Thinking Publishing**

### Other Books about the Social Thinking Model & Curriculum
*Worksheets for Teaching Social Thinking and Related Skills*
*Social Behavior Mapping: Connecting Behavior, Emotions and Consequences Across the Day* *

### For School-Age Children
*You Are a Social Detective!* (co-authored by Pamela Crooke) **
*Superflex... A Superhero Social Thinking Curriculum* (co-authored by Stephanie Madrigal)
*Superflex Takes on Rock Brain and the Team of Unthinkables* By Stephanie Madrigal
*Superflex Takes on Glassman* (co-authored by Stephanie Madrigal)
*Superflex Takes on Brain Eater* (co-authored by Stephanie Madrigal)
*Social Town Citizens Discover 82 New Unthinkables for Superflex to Outsmart*
(co-authored by Stephanie Madrigal and Pamela Crooke)
*Sticker Strategies: Practical Strategies to Encourage Social Thinking and Organization, 2nd Edition*
*Whole Body Listening Larry at Home!* By Kristen Wilson & Elizabeth Sautter
*Whole Body Listening Larry at School!* By Elizabeth Sautter & Kristen Wilson
*We Can Make it Better! A Strategy to Motivate and Engage Young Learners in Social Problem-Solving Through Flexible Stories* By Elizabeth M. Delsandro
*I Get It! Building Social Thinking and Reading Comprehension Through Book Chats* By Audra Jensen, M.Ed., BCBA
*The Zones of Regulation: A Curriculum Designed to Foster Self-Regulation and Emotional Control* By Leah M. Kuypers, MA Ed., OTR/L
*What is a Thought? (A Thought is a Lot)* By Jack Pransky and Amy Kahofer
*Movie Time Social Learning* by Anna Vagin, PhD

* Available in English and Spanish    ** Available in English, French, and Spanish

## Teens and Young Adults

*Socially Curious and Curiously Social: A Social Thinking Guidebook for Teens and Young Adults*
(co-authored by Pamela Crooke)
*Social Fortune or Social Fate: Watch Their Destiny Unfold Based on the Choices They Make*
(co-authored by Pamela Crooke)
*Social Thinking Worksheets for Tweens and Teens: Learning to Read in Between the Social Lines*
*Social Thinking Across the Home and School Day*
*Strategies for Organization: Preparing for Homework and the Real World*
*Social Thinking at Work: Why Should I Care? A Guidebook for Understanding
and Navigating the Social Complexities of the Workplace*
(co-authored by Pamela Crooke)
*Should I or Shouldn't I? What Would Others Think?*
*Middle & High School Edition (game)* By Dominique Baudry, MS., Ed.

## Related Products

*You Are a Social Detective Interactive CD*
*Social Thinking Posters for the home and classroom*
*The Zones of Regulation Poster*
*Superflex Poster*
*Whole Body Listening Larry Poster*

**Visit our website for more information on our books and products, free articles on Social Thinking topics, and a listing of Social Thinking Conferences across the U.S.**

**www.socialthinking.com**